W9-BCO-499

STAR WARS®

THE CLONE WARS™

IN SERVICE OF THE REPUBLIC
VOLUME THREE

BLOOD AND SNOW

SCRIPT
HENRY GILROY
STEVEN MELCHING

PENCILS
SCOTT HEPBURN

INKS
DAN PARSONS

COLORS
MICHAEL E. WIGGAM

LETTERING
MICHAEL HEISLER

COVER ART
BRIAN KALIN O'CONNELL

The frozen world of Khorm is the setting for a fierce struggle between clone and droid armies desperate to secure access to a rare and powerful ore. Republic troops have won significant victories over their adversaries, but the incompetence of the overzealous Republic officer Captain Kendal Ozzel, combined with the arrival of Separatist commander Asajj Ventress have led to some setbacks.

Fortunately, Jedi Masters Plo Koon and Kit Fisto and their clone commandos successfully destroyed the Separatist weather-control station, allowing Republic reinforcements to arrive from orbit in time to save Ozzel and his troops.

With the Separatist forces in retreat, Plo and Kit scout the agrocite mine in preparation for an all-out assault . . .

Spotlight

DARK HORSE COMICS

GN
STAR WARS

Visit us at www.abdopublishing.com

Reinforced library bound edition published in 2011 by Spotlight, a division of the ABDO Group, 8000 West 78th Street, Edina, Minnesota 55439. Spotlight produces high-quality reinforced library bound editions for schools and libraries. Published by agreement with Dark Horse Comics, Inc., and Lucasfilm Ltd.

Printed in the United States of America, North Mankato, Minnesota.
102010
012011
♻This book contains at least 10% recycled materials.

Cataloging-in-Publication Data

Gilroy, Henry.
 In service of the Republic Vol. 3: blood and snow / story, Henry Gilroy and Steve Melching ; art, Scott Hepburn. --Reinforced library bound ed.
    v. cm. -- (Star wars: the clone wars)
    "Dark Horse Comics."
 ISBN 978-1-59961-840-1 (v. 3)
 1. Graphic novels. [1. Graphic novels.] I. Melching, Steve. II. Hepburn, Scott, ill. III. Star Wars, the clone wars (television program) IV. Title.
 PZ7.7.G55Se 2011
 741.5'973

All Spotlight books have reinforced library bindings and are manufactured in the United States of America.

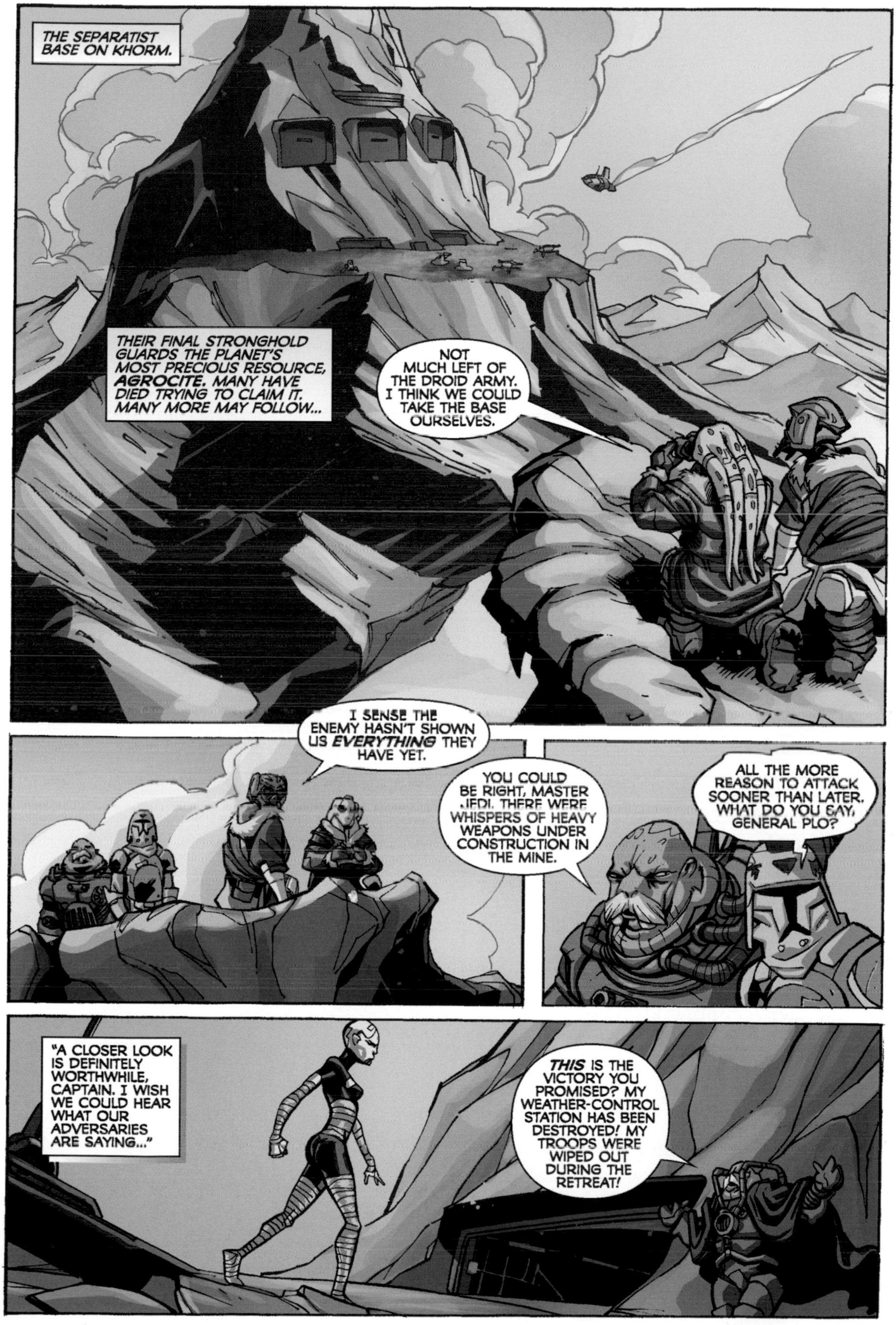
THE SEPARATIST BASE ON KHORM.
THEIR FINAL STRONGHOLD GUARDS THE PLANET'S MOST PRECIOUS RESOURCE, AGROCITE. MANY HAVE DIED TRYING TO CLAIM IT. MANY MORE MAY FOLLOW...
NOT MUCH LEFT OF THE DROID ARMY. I THINK WE COULD TAKE THE BASE OURSELVES.
I SENSE THE ENEMY HASN'T SHOWN US EVERYTHING THEY HAVE YET.
YOU COULD BE RIGHT, MASTER JEDI. THERE WERE WHISPERS OF HEAVY WEAPONS UNDER CONSTRUCTION IN THE MINE.
ALL THE MORE REASON TO ATTACK SOONER THAN LATER. WHAT DO YOU SAY, GENERAL PLO?
"A CLOSER LOOK IS DEFINITELY WORTHWHILE, CAPTAIN. I WISH WE COULD HEAR WHAT OUR ADVERSARIES ARE SAYING..."
THIS IS THE VICTORY YOU PROMISED? MY WEATHER-CONTROL STATION HAS BEEN DESTROYED! MY TROOPS WERE WIPED OUT DURING THE RETREAT!

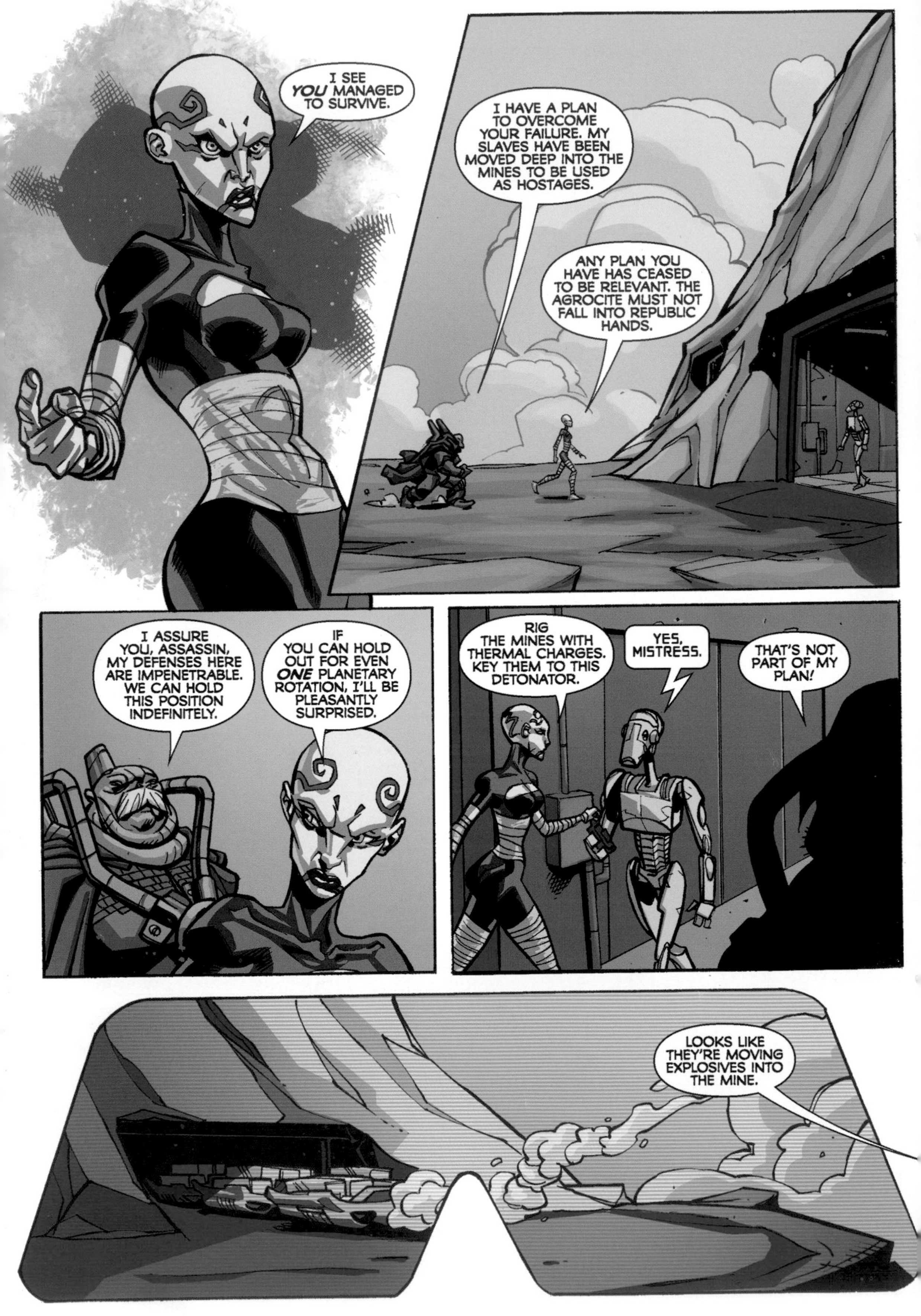
I SEE YOU MANAGED TO SURVIVE.
I HAVE A PLAN TO OVERCOME YOUR FAILURE. MY SLAVES HAVE BEEN MOVED DEEP INTO THE MINES TO BE USED AS HOSTAGES.
ANY PLAN YOU HAVE HAS CEASED TO BE RELEVANT. THE AGROCITE MUST NOT FALL INTO REPUBLIC HANDS.
I ASSURE YOU, ASSASSIN, MY DEFENSES HERE ARE IMPENETRABLE. WE CAN HOLD THIS POSITION INDEFINITELY.
IF YOU CAN HOLD OUT FOR EVEN ONE PLANETARY ROTATION, I'LL BE PLEASANTLY SURPRISED.
RIG THE MINES WITH THERMAL CHARGES. KEY THEM TO THIS DETONATOR.
YES, MISTRESS.
THAT'S NOT PART OF MY PLAN!
LOOKS LIKE THEY'RE MOVING EXPLOSIVES INTO THE MINE.

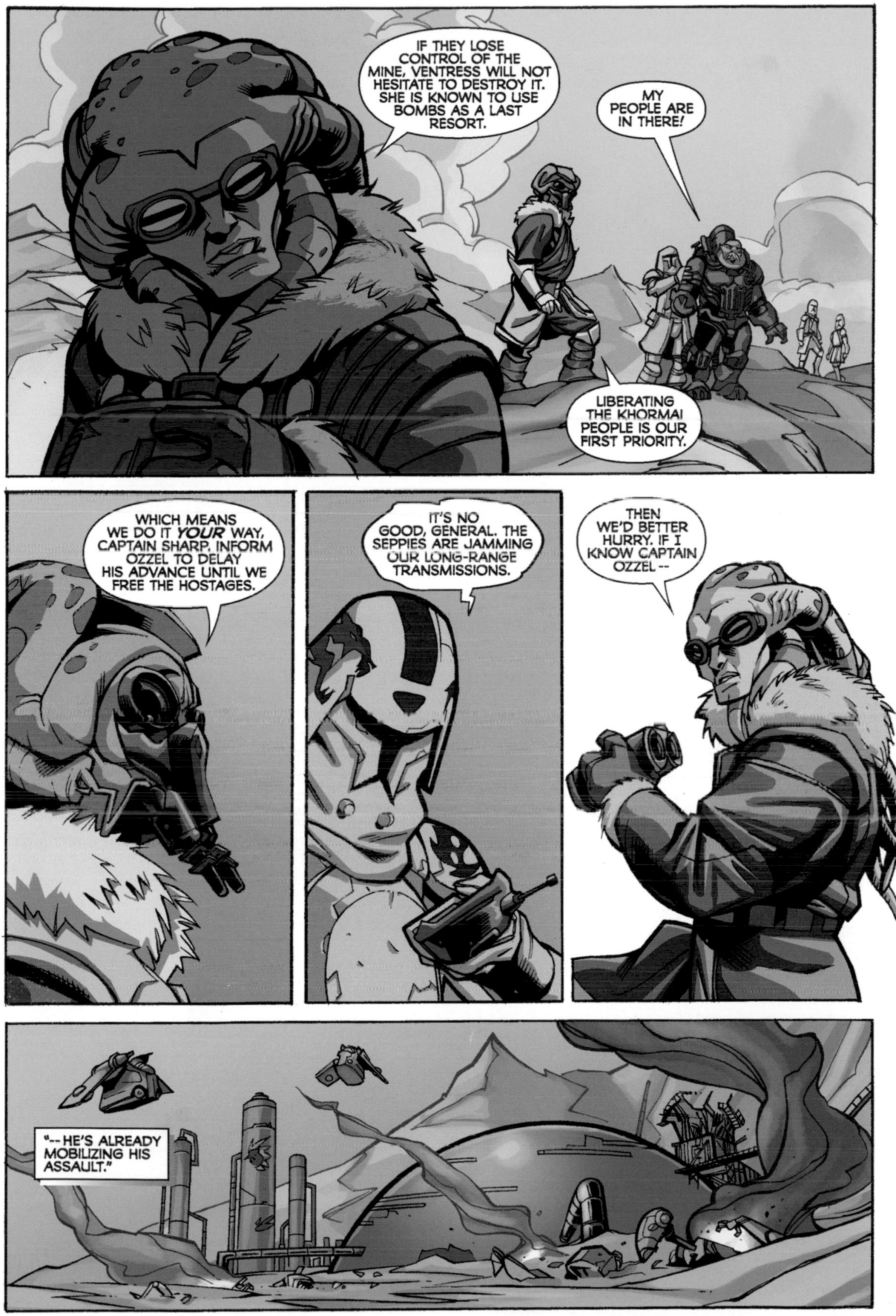
IF THEY LOSE CONTROL OF THE MINE, VENTRESS WILL NOT HESITATE TO DESTROY IT. SHE IS KNOWN TO USE BOMBS AS A LAST RESORT.
MY PEOPLE ARE IN THERE!
LIBERATING THE KHORMAI PEOPLE IS OUR FIRST PRIORITY.
WHICH MEANS WE DO IT *YOUR* WAY, CAPTAIN SHARP. INFORM OZZEL TO DELAY HIS ADVANCE UNTIL WE FREE THE HOSTAGES.
IT'S NO GOOD, GENERAL. THE SEPPIES ARE JAMMING OUR LONG-RANGE TRANSMISSIONS.
THEN WE'D BETTER HURRY. IF I KNOW CAPTAIN OZZEL --
"-- HE'S ALREADY MOBILIZING HIS ASSAULT."

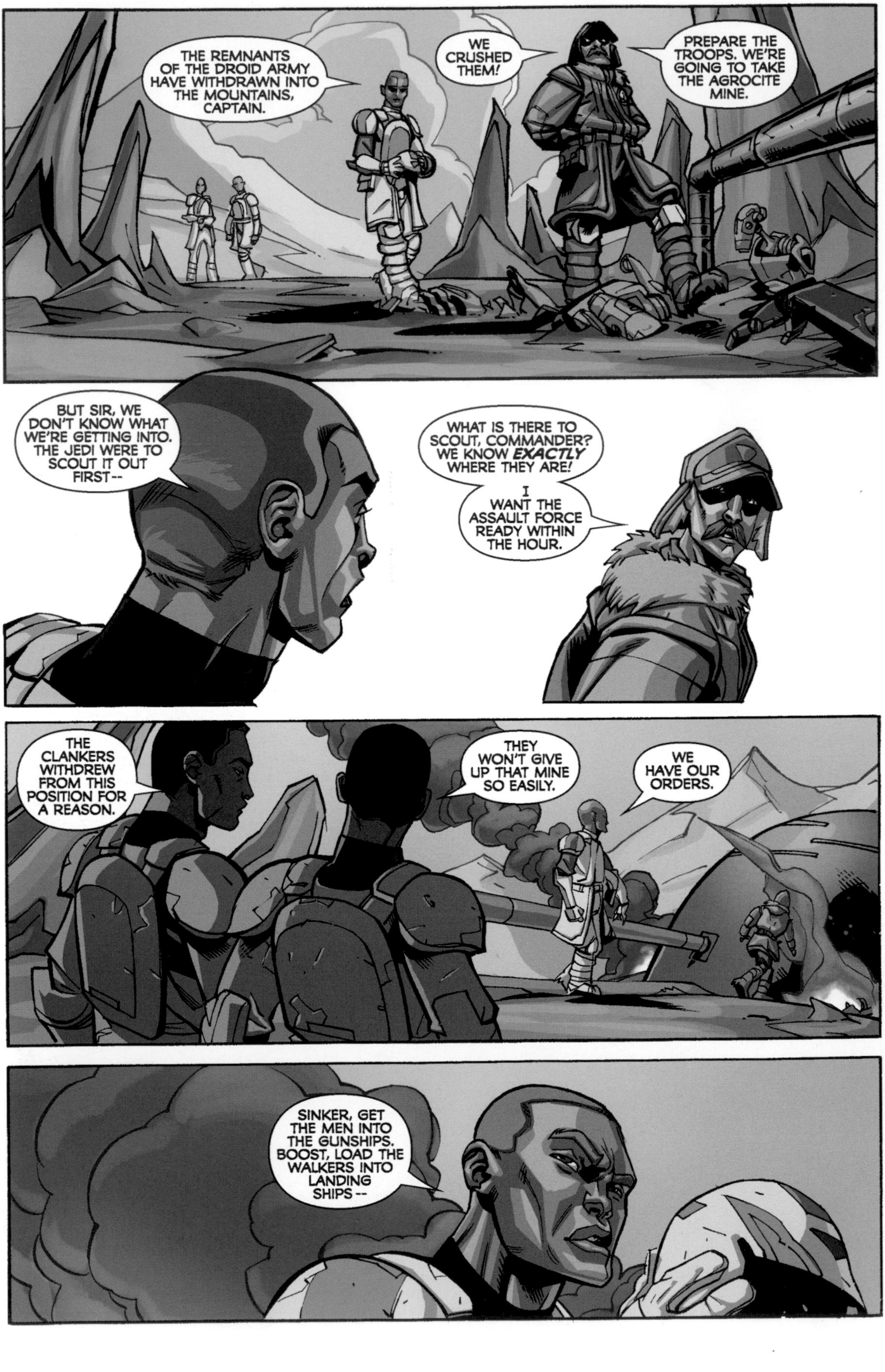
THE REMNANTS OF THE DROID ARMY HAVE WITHDRAWN INTO THE MOUNTAINS, CAPTAIN.
WE CRUSHED THEM!
PREPARE THE TROOPS. WE'RE GOING TO TAKE THE AGROCITE MINE.
BUT SIR, WE DON'T KNOW WHAT WE'RE GETTING INTO. THE JEDI WERE TO SCOUT IT OUT FIRST--
WHAT IS THERE TO SCOUT, COMMANDER? WE KNOW *EXACTLY* WHERE THEY ARE!
I WANT THE ASSAULT FORCE READY WITHIN THE HOUR.
THE CLANKERS WITHDREW FROM THIS POSITION FOR A REASON.
THEY WON'T GIVE UP THAT MINE SO EASILY.
WE HAVE OUR ORDERS.
SINKER, GET THE MEN INTO THE GUNSHIPS. BOOST, LOAD THE WALKERS INTO LANDING SHIPS--

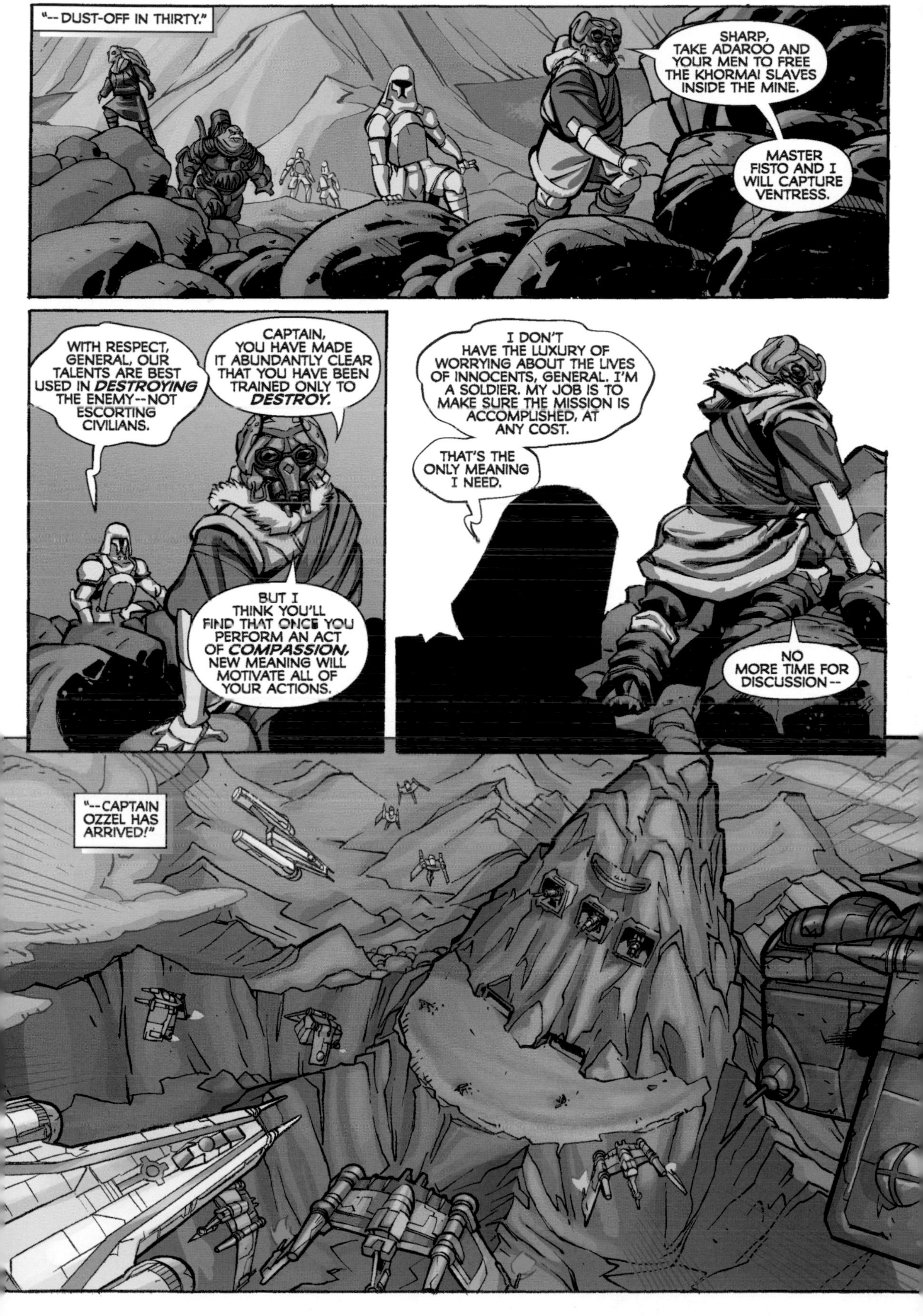
"-- DUST-OFF IN THIRTY."
SHARP, TAKE ADAROO AND YOUR MEN TO FREE THE KHORMAI SLAVES INSIDE THE MINE.
MASTER FISTO AND I WILL CAPTURE VENTRESS.
WITH RESPECT, GENERAL, OUR TALENTS ARE BEST USED IN DESTROYING THE ENEMY--NOT ESCORTING CIVILIANS.
CAPTAIN, YOU HAVE MADE IT ABUNDANTLY CLEAR THAT YOU HAVE BEEN TRAINED ONLY TO DESTROY.
BUT I THINK YOU'LL FIND THAT ONCE YOU PERFORM AN ACT OF COMPASSION, NEW MEANING WILL MOTIVATE ALL OF YOUR ACTIONS.
I DON'T HAVE THE LUXURY OF WORRYING ABOUT THE LIVES OF INNOCENTS, GENERAL. I'M A SOLDIER. MY JOB IS TO MAKE SURE THE MISSION IS ACCOMPLISHED, AT ANY COST.
THAT'S THE ONLY MEANING I NEED.
NO MORE TIME FOR DISCUSSION --
"--CAPTAIN OZZEL HAS ARRIVED!"

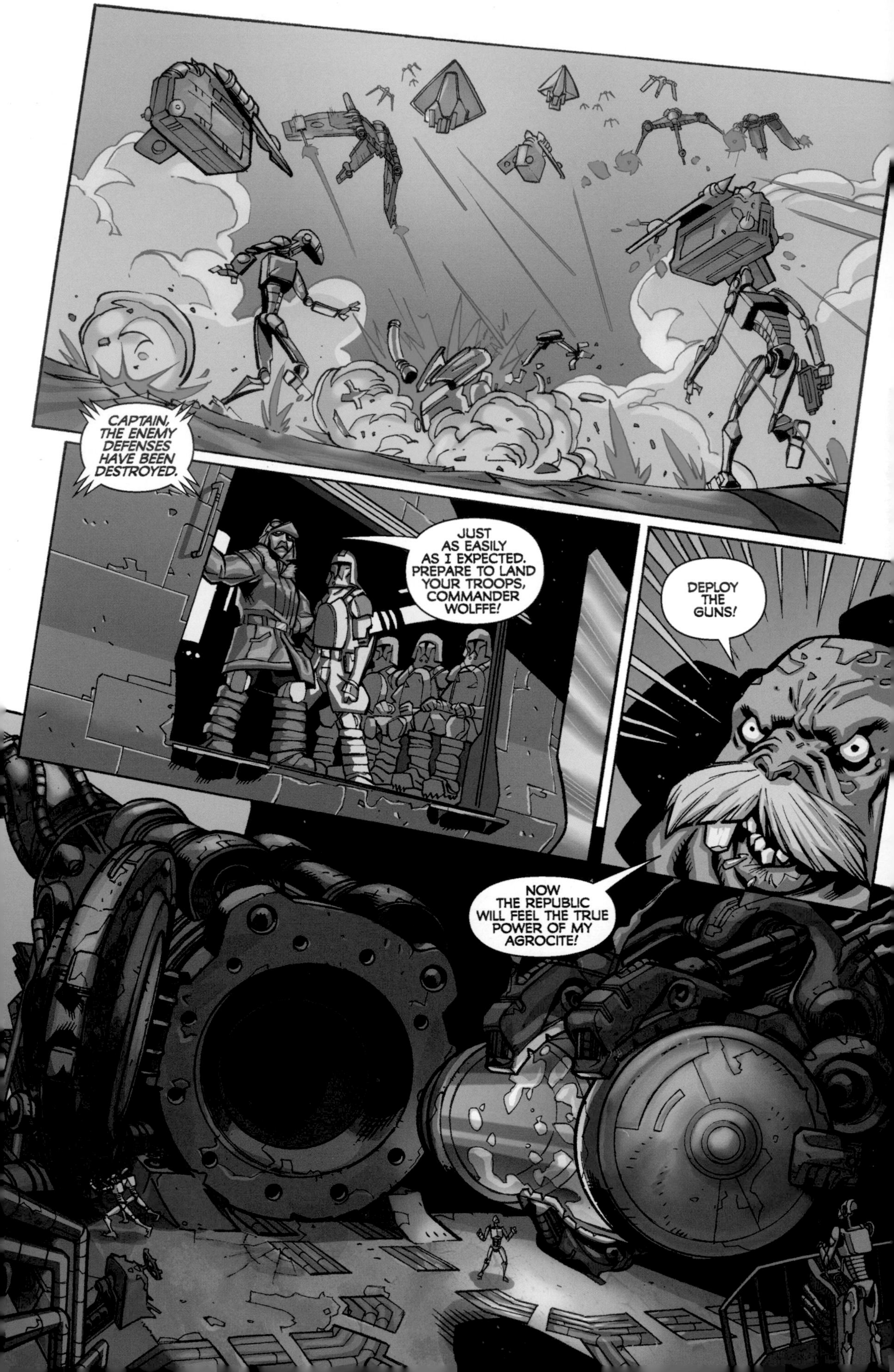
CAPTAIN, THE ENEMY DEFENSES HAVE BEEN DESTROYED.
JUST AS EASILY AS I EXPECTED. PREPARE TO LAND YOUR TROOPS, COMMANDER WOLFFE!
DEPLOY THE GUNS!
NOW THE REPUBLIC WILL FEEL THE TRUE POWER OF MY AGROCITE!

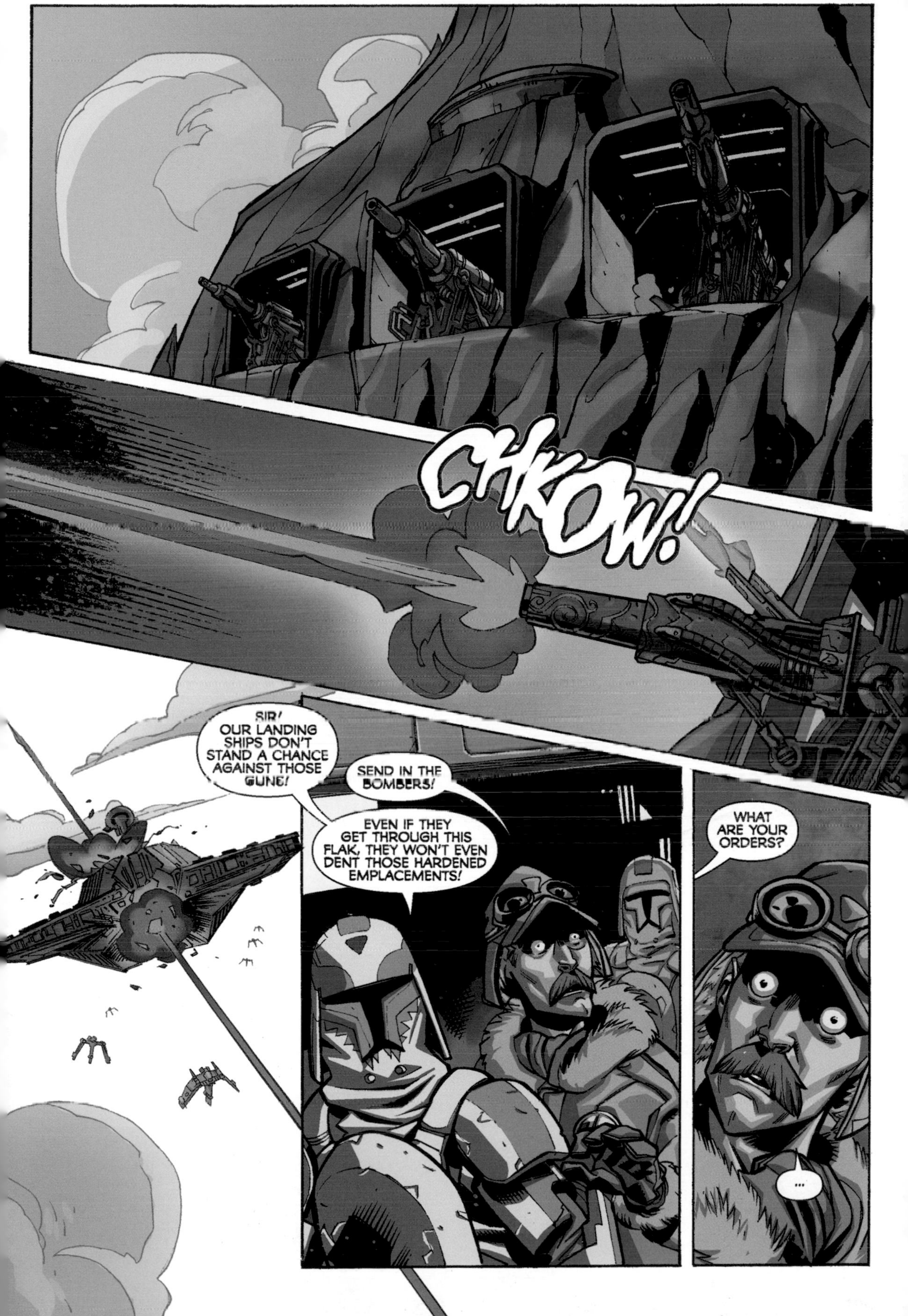
CHKOW!!
SIR! OUR LANDING SHIPS DON'T STAND A CHANCE AGAINST THOSE GUNS!
SEND IN THE BOMBERS!
EVEN IF THEY GET THROUGH THIS FLAK, THEY WON'T EVEN DENT THOSE HARDENED EMPLACEMENTS!
WHAT ARE YOUR ORDERS?
...

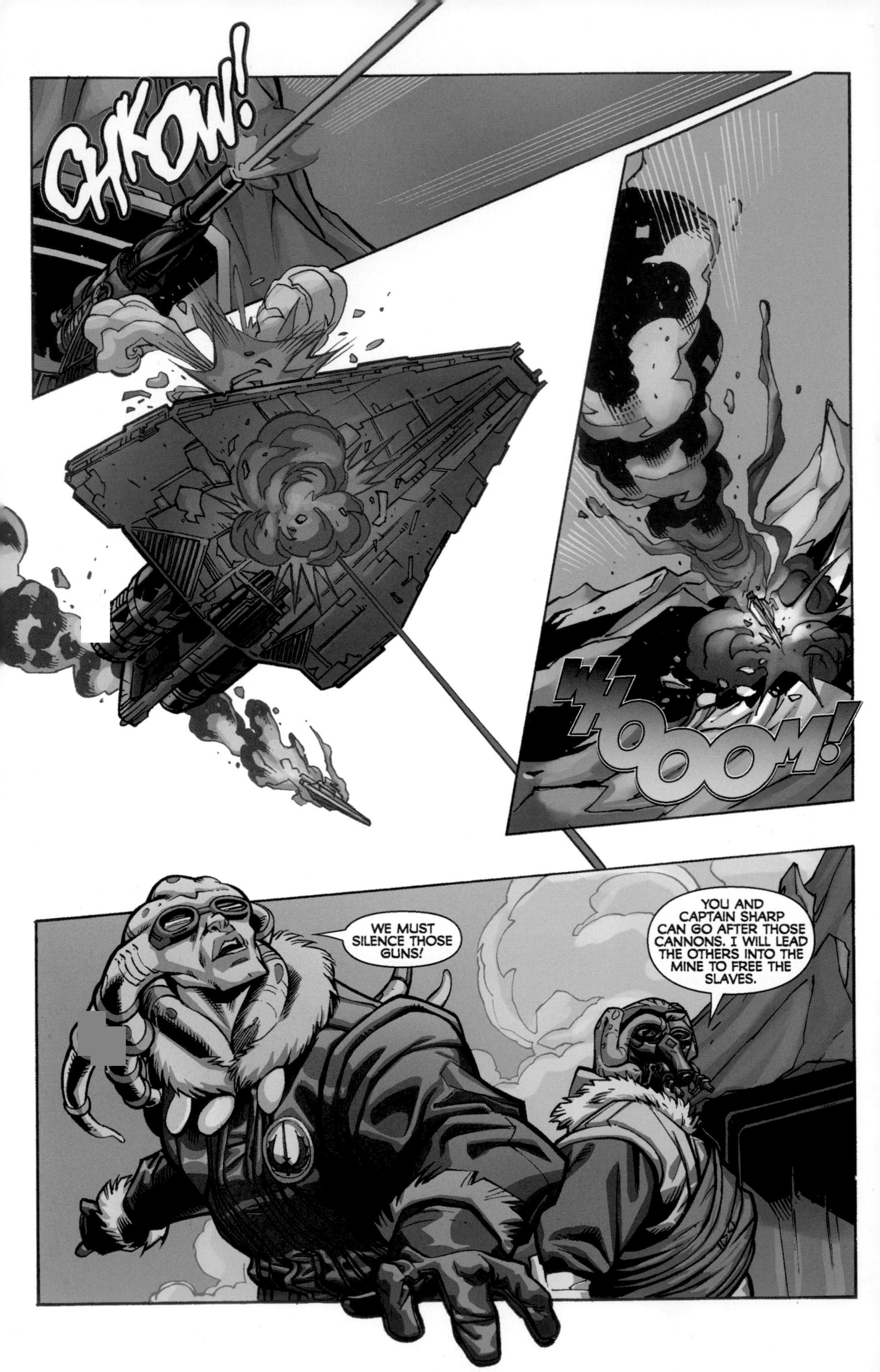
CHKOW!
WHOOOOM!
WE MUST SILENCE THOSE GUNS!
YOU AND CAPTAIN SHARP CAN GO AFTER THOSE CANNONS. I WILL LEAD THE OTHERS INTO THE MINE TO FREE THE SLAVES.

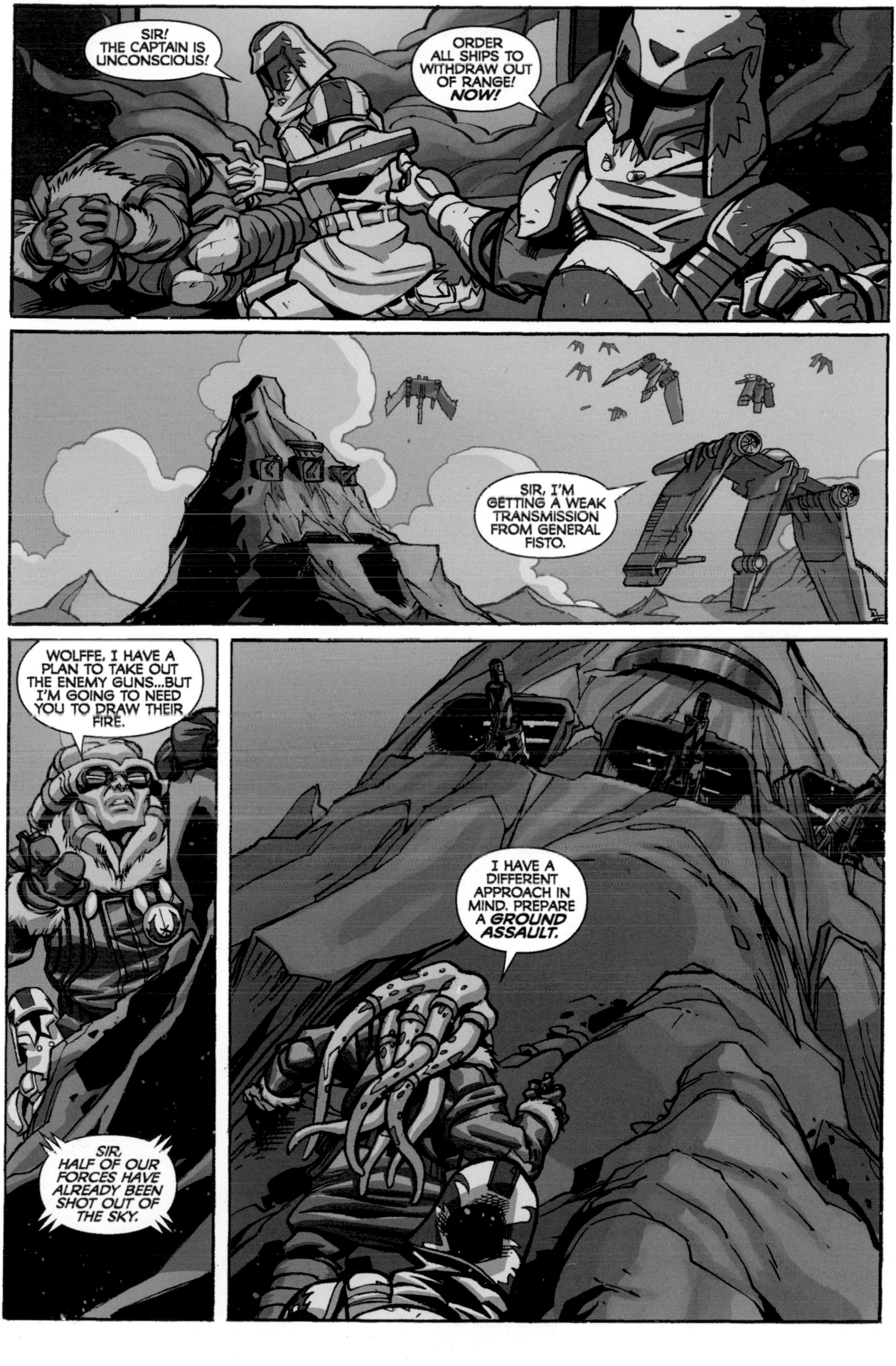
SIR! THE CAPTAIN IS UNCONSCIOUS!
ORDER ALL SHIPS TO WITHDRAW OUT OF RANGE! NOW!
SIR, I'M GETTING A WEAK TRANSMISSION FROM GENERAL FISTO.
WOLFFE, I HAVE A PLAN TO TAKE OUT THE ENEMY GUNS...BUT I'M GOING TO NEED YOU TO DRAW THEIR FIRE.
SIR, HALF OF OUR FORCES HAVE ALREADY BEEN SHOT OUT OF THE SKY.
I HAVE A DIFFERENT APPROACH IN MIND. PREPARE A GROUND ASSAULT.

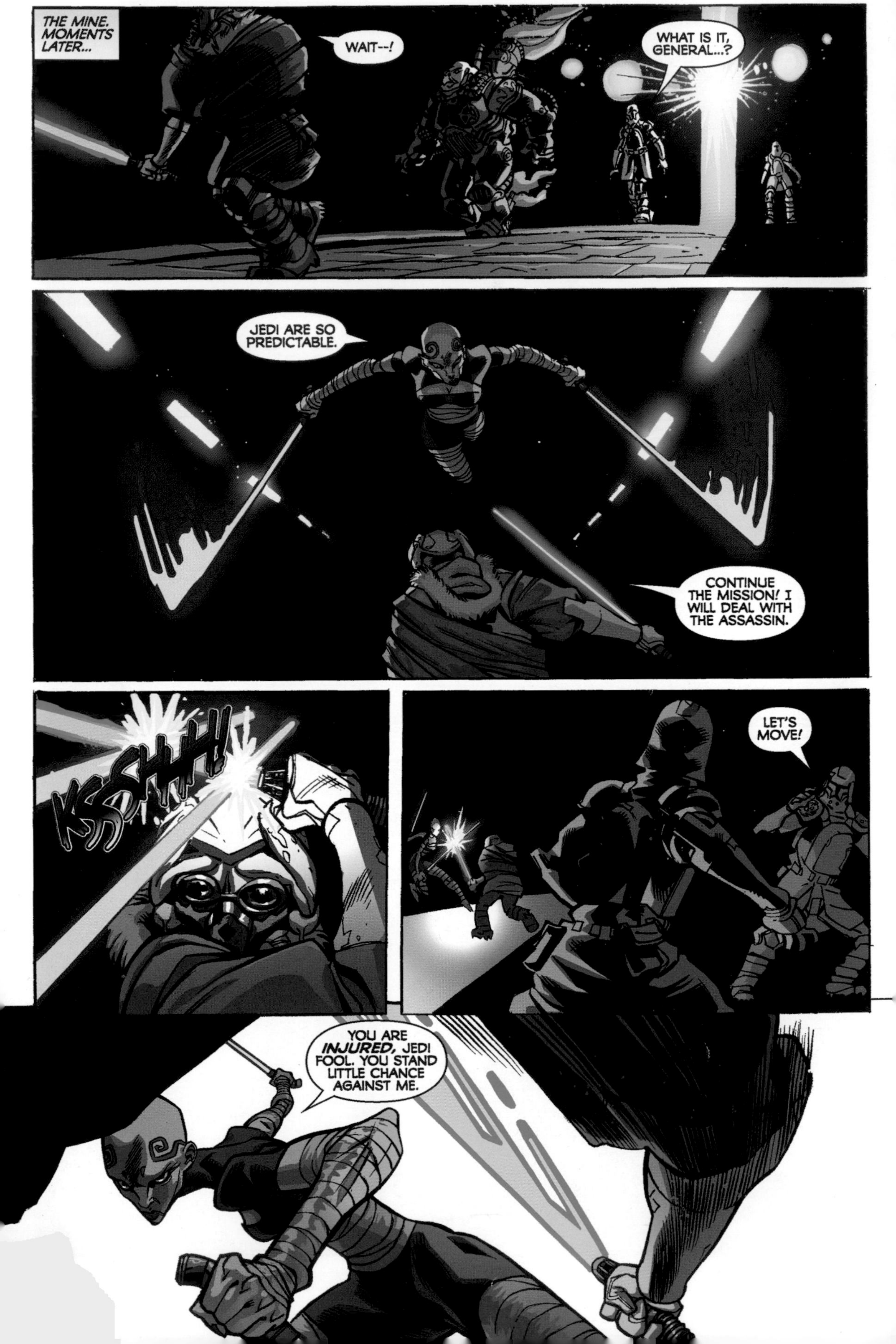
THE MINE. MOMENTS LATER...
WAIT--!
WHAT IS IT, GENERAL...?
JEDI ARE SO PREDICTABLE.
CONTINUE THE MISSION! I WILL DEAL WITH THE ASSASSIN.
KSSHHH!
LET'S MOVE!
YOU ARE *INJURED,* JEDI FOOL. YOU STAND LITTLE CHANCE AGAINST ME.

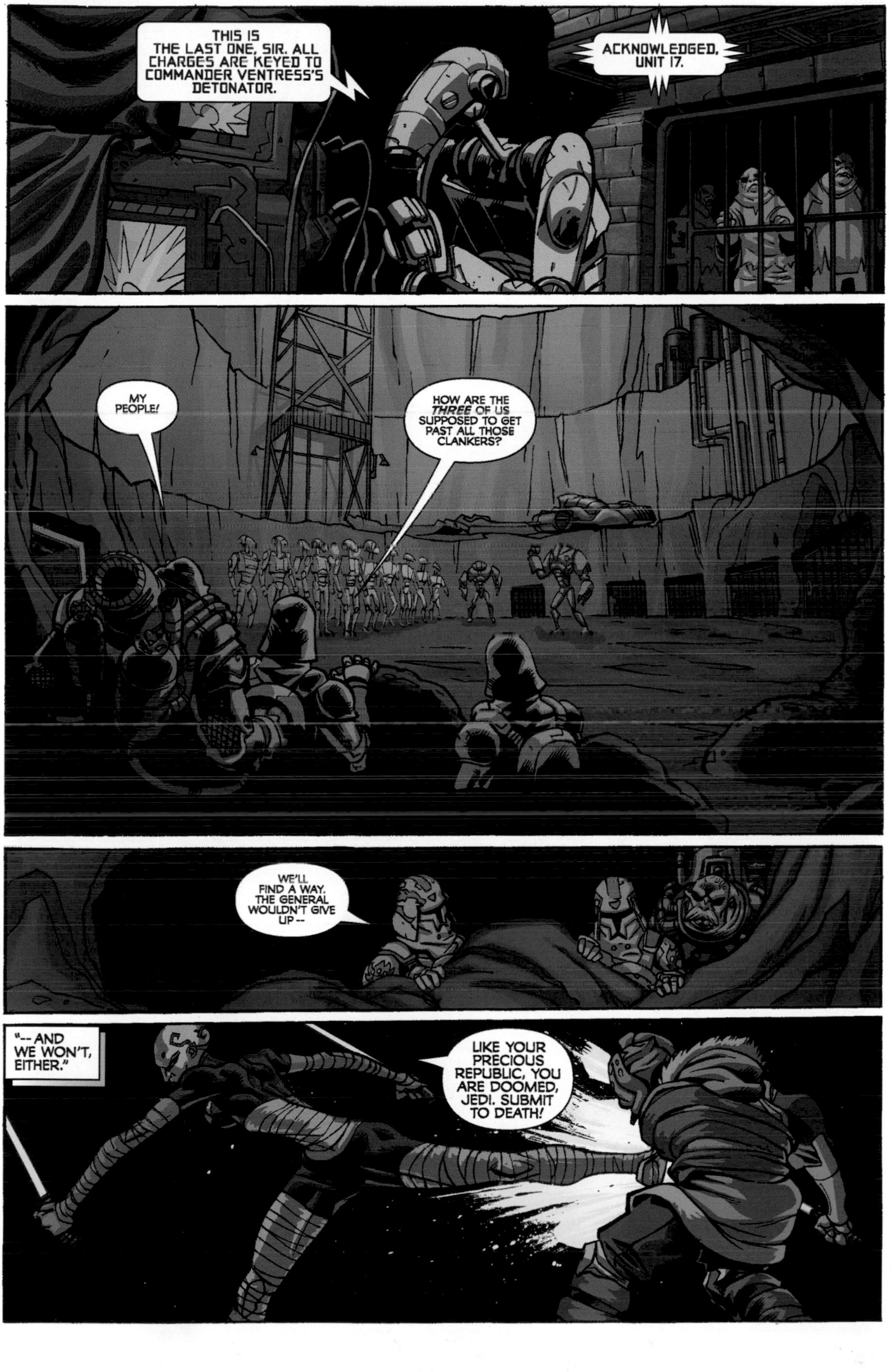
THIS IS THE LAST ONE, SIR. ALL CHARGES ARE KEYED TO COMMANDER VENTRESS'S DETONATOR.
ACKNOWLEDGED, UNIT 17.
MY PEOPLE!
HOW ARE THE *THREE* OF US SUPPOSED TO GET PAST ALL THOSE CLANKERS?
WE'LL FIND A WAY. THE GENERAL WOULDN'T GIVE UP--
"--AND WE WON'T, EITHER."
LIKE YOUR PRECIOUS REPUBLIC, YOU ARE DOOMED, JEDI. SUBMIT TO DEATH!

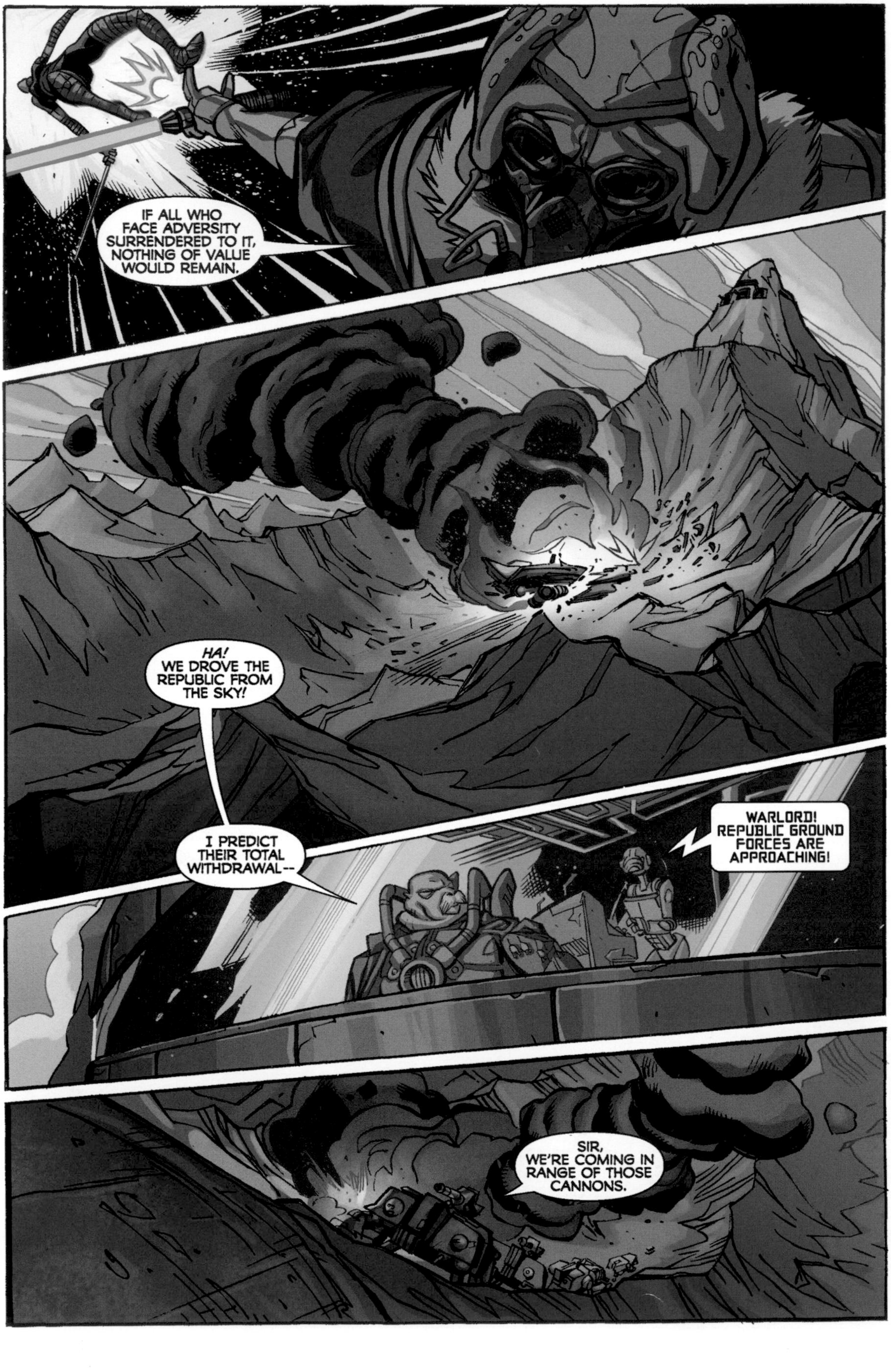
IF ALL WHO FACE ADVERSITY SURRENDERED TO IT, NOTHING OF VALUE WOULD REMAIN.
HA! WE DROVE THE REPUBLIC FROM THE SKY!
I PREDICT THEIR TOTAL WITHDRAWAL--
WARLORD! REPUBLIC GROUND FORCES ARE APPROACHING!
SIR, WE'RE COMING IN RANGE OF THOSE CANNONS.

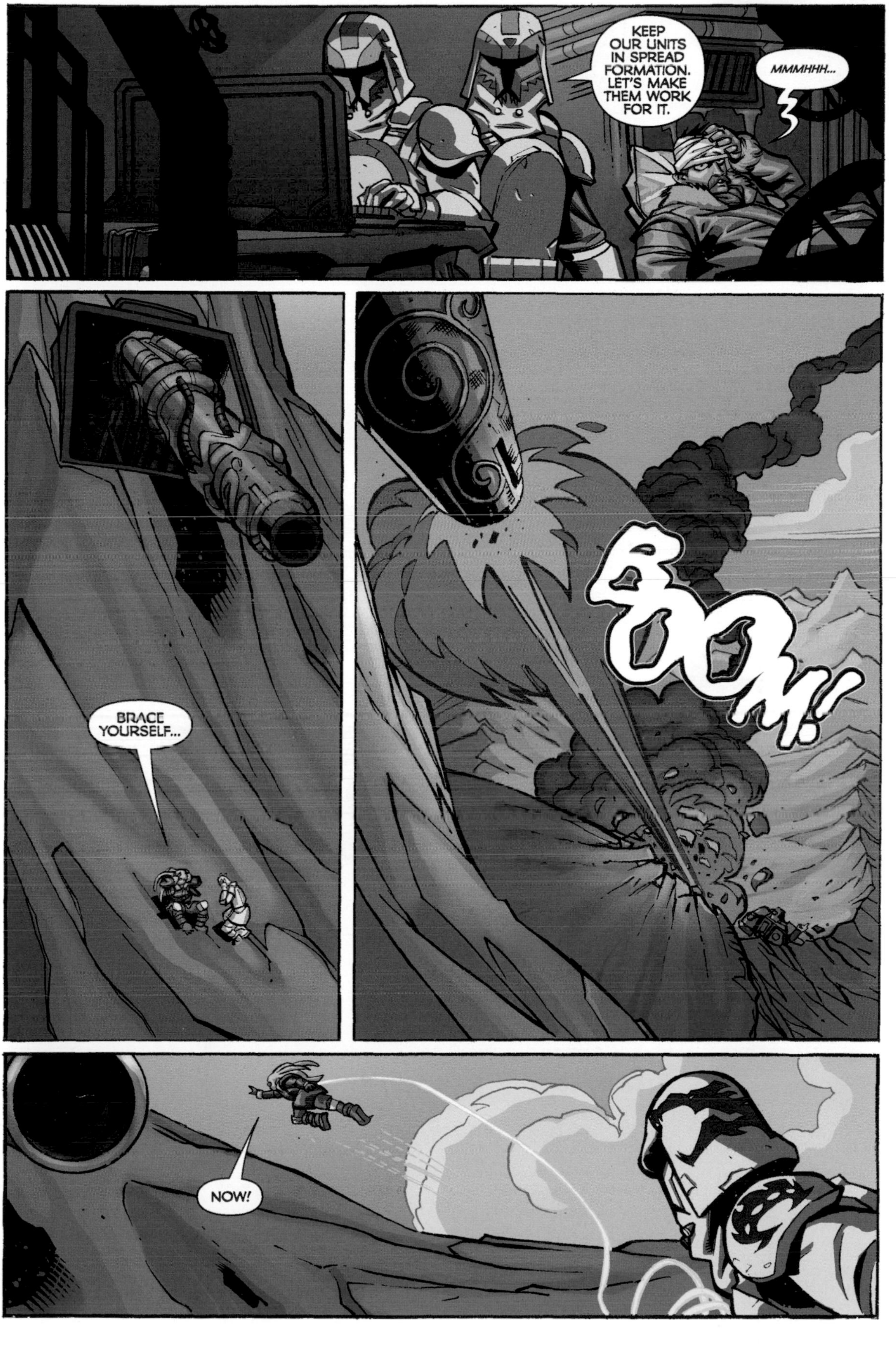
KEEP OUR UNITS IN SPREAD FORMATION. LET'S MAKE THEM WORK FOR IT.
MMMHHH...
BRACE YOURSELF...
BOOM!!
NOW!

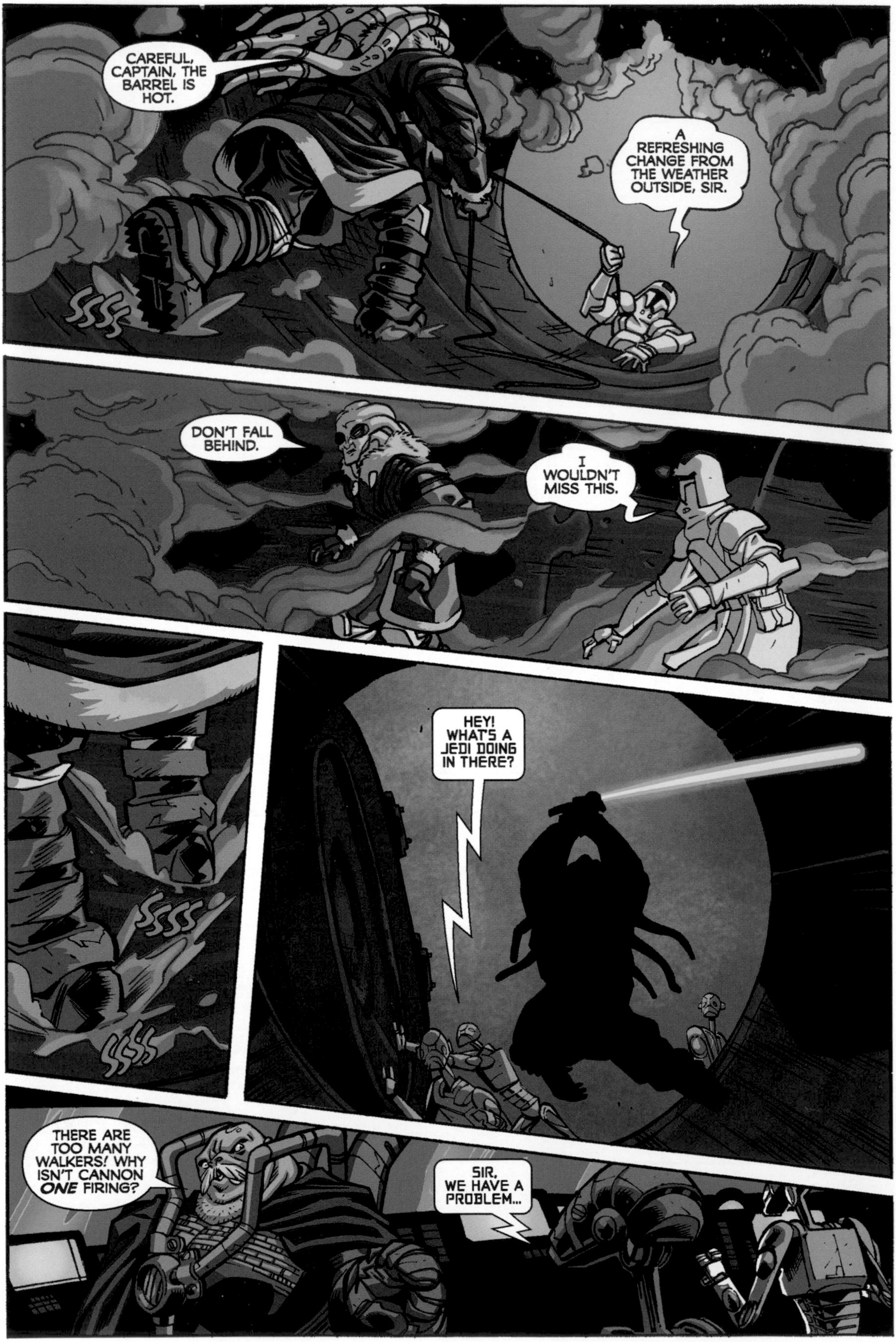
CAREFUL, CAPTAIN, THE BARREL IS HOT.
A REFRESHING CHANGE FROM THE WEATHER OUTSIDE, SIR.
DON'T FALL BEHIND.
I WOULDN'T MISS THIS.
HEY! WHAT'S A JEDI DOING IN THERE?
SSSS
SSSS
THERE ARE TOO MANY WALKERS! WHY ISN'T CANNON ONE FIRING?
SIR, WE HAVE A PROBLEM...

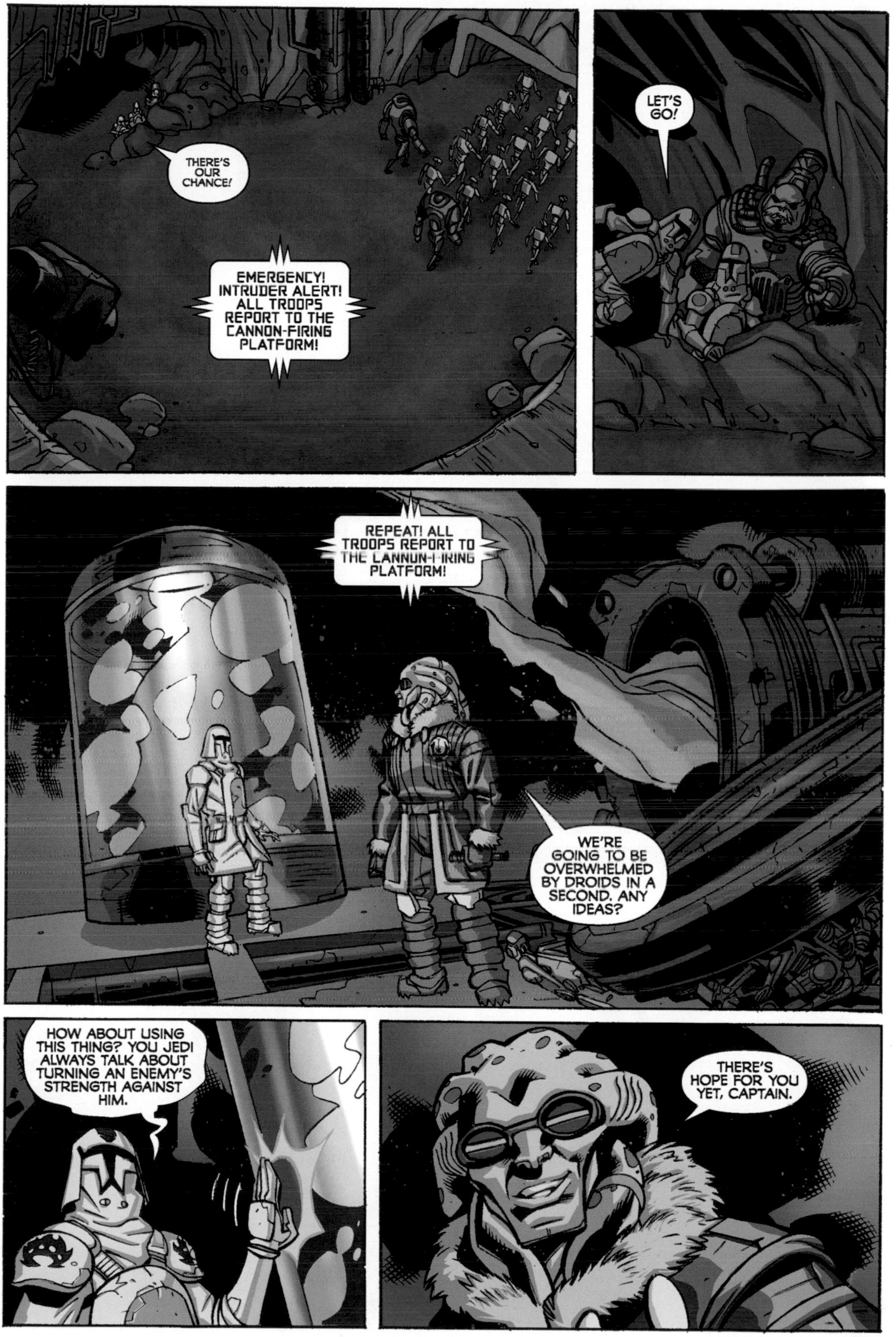
THERE'S OUR CHANCE!
EMERGENCY! INTRUDER ALERT! ALL TROOPS REPORT TO THE CANNON-FIRING PLATFORM!
LET'S GO!
REPEAT! ALL TROOPS REPORT TO THE CANNON-FIRING PLATFORM!
WE'RE GOING TO BE OVERWHELMED BY DROIDS IN A SECOND. ANY IDEAS?
HOW ABOUT USING THIS THING? YOU JEDI ALWAYS TALK ABOUT TURNING AN ENEMY'S STRENGTH AGAINST HIM.
THERE'S HOPE FOR YOU YET, CAPTAIN.

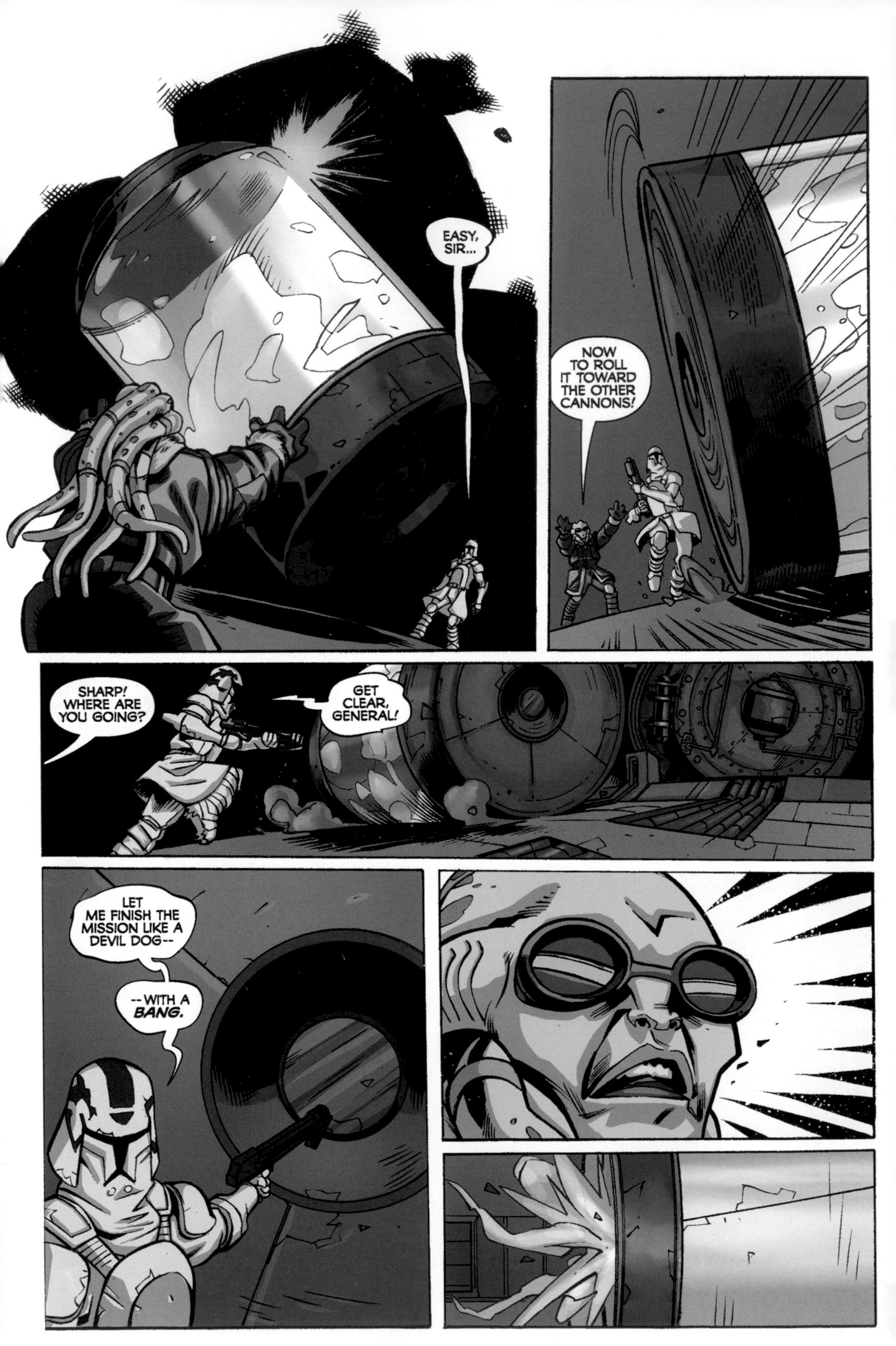
EASY, SIR...
NOW TO ROLL IT TOWARD THE OTHER CANNONS!
SHARP! WHERE ARE YOU GOING?
GET CLEAR, GENERAL!
LET ME FINISH THE MISSION LIKE A DEVIL DOG--
--WITH A *BANG.*

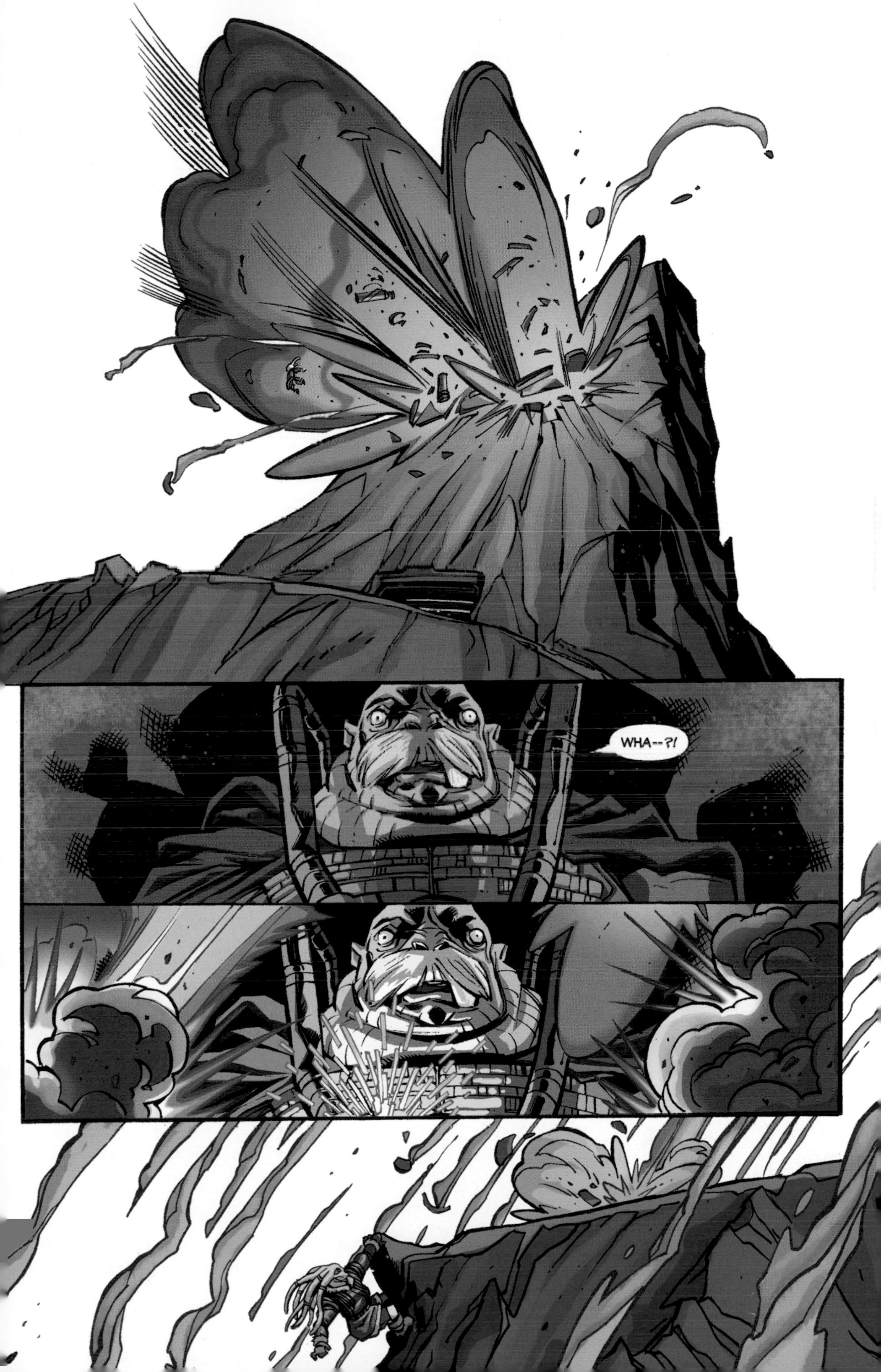
WHA--?!

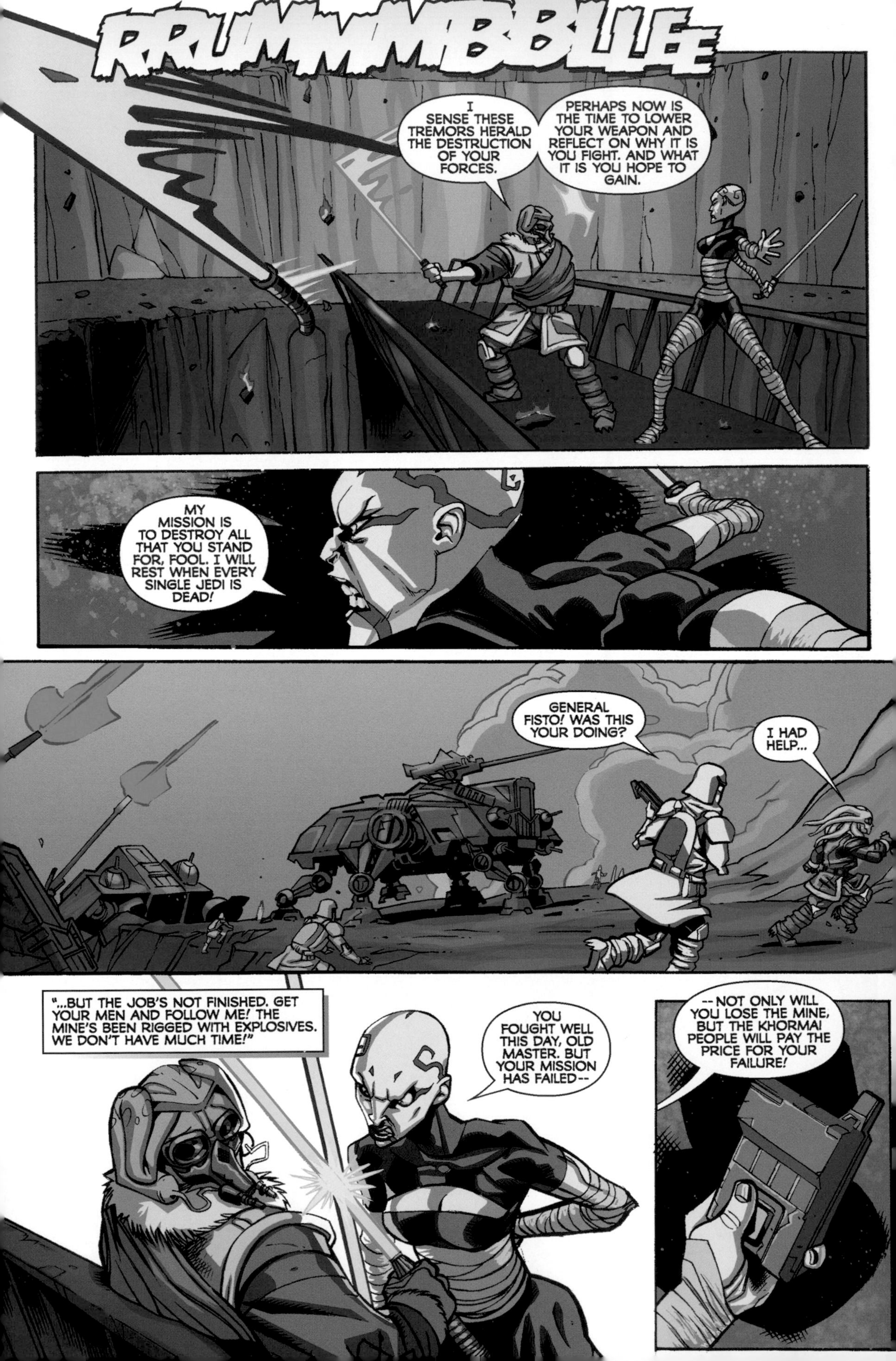
RRUMMMBBLLEE
I SENSE THESE TREMORS HERALD THE DESTRUCTION OF YOUR FORCES.
PERHAPS NOW IS THE TIME TO LOWER YOUR WEAPON AND REFLECT ON WHY IT IS YOU FIGHT. AND WHAT IT IS YOU HOPE TO GAIN.
MY MISSION IS TO DESTROY ALL THAT YOU STAND FOR, FOOL. I WILL REST WHEN EVERY SINGLE JEDI IS DEAD!
GENERAL FISTO! WAS THIS YOUR DOING?
I HAD HELP...
"...BUT THE JOB'S NOT FINISHED. GET YOUR MEN AND FOLLOW ME! THE MINE'S BEEN RIGGED WITH EXPLOSIVES. WE DON'T HAVE MUCH TIME!"
YOU FOUGHT WELL THIS DAY, OLD MASTER. BUT YOUR MISSION HAS FAILED--
--NOT ONLY WILL YOU LOSE THE MINE, BUT THE KHORMAI PEOPLE WILL PAY THE PRICE FOR YOUR FAILURE!

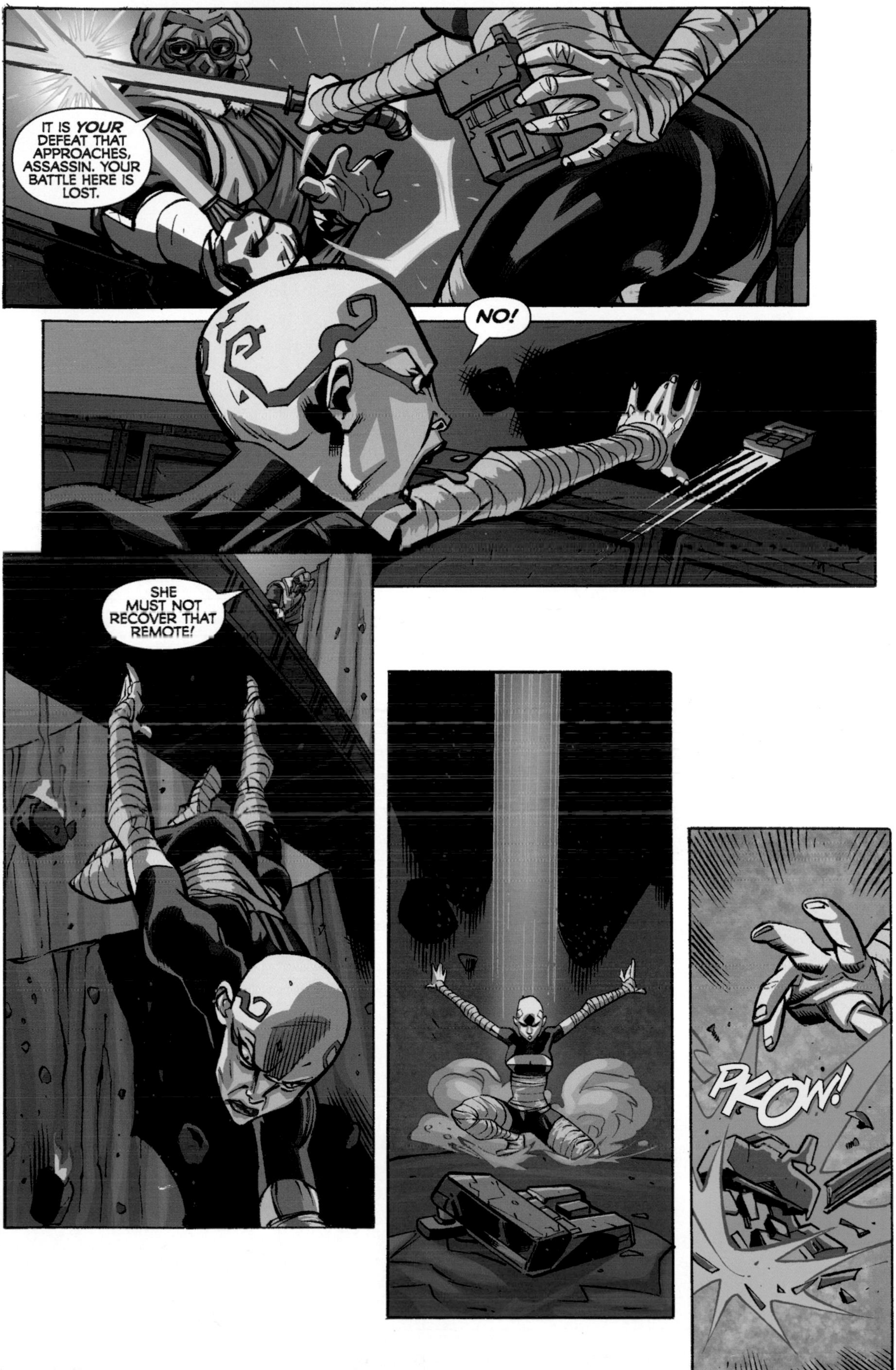
IT IS *YOUR* DEFEAT THAT APPROACHES, ASSASSIN. YOUR BATTLE HERE IS LOST.
NO!
SHE MUST NOT RECOVER THAT REMOTE!
PKOW!

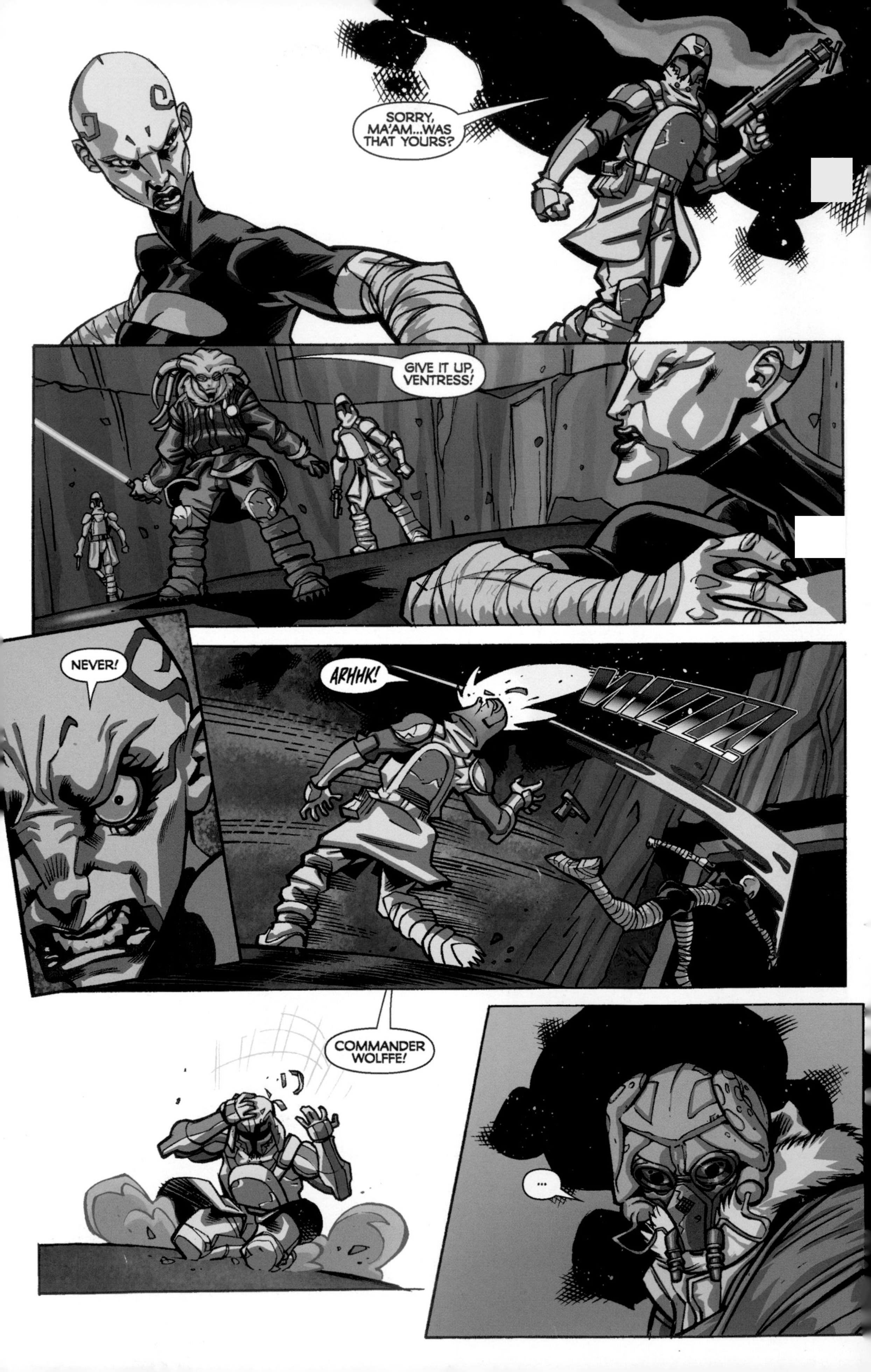
SORRY, MA'AM...WAS THAT YOURS?
GIVE IT UP, VENTRESS!
NEVER!
ARHHK!
VHZZZZ!
COMMANDER WOLFFE!
...

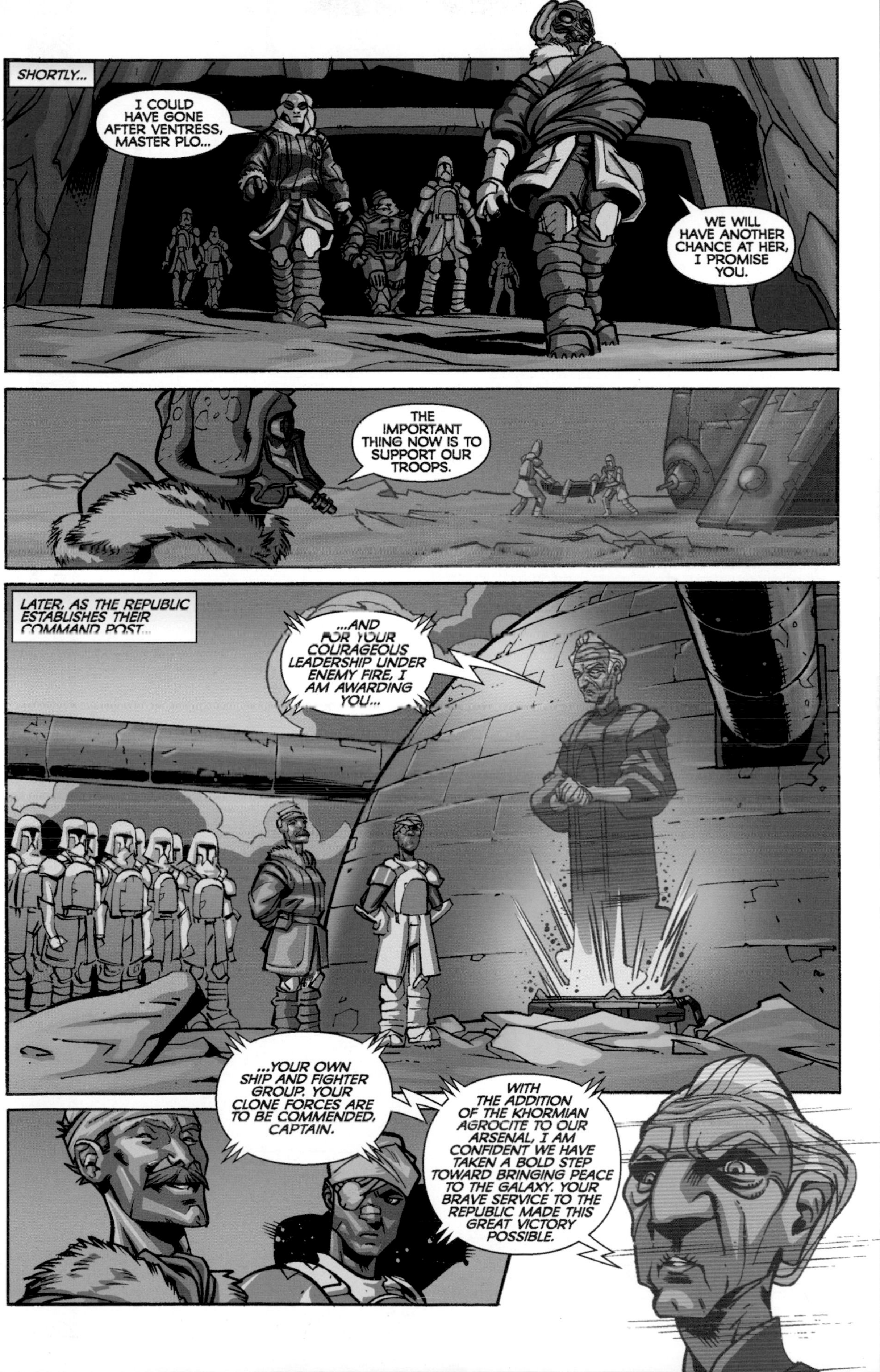
SHORTLY...
I COULD HAVE GONE AFTER VENTRESS, MASTER PLO...
WE WILL HAVE ANOTHER CHANCE AT HER, I PROMISE YOU.
THE IMPORTANT THING NOW IS TO SUPPORT OUR TROOPS.
LATER, AS THE REPUBLIC ESTABLISHES THEIR COMMAND POST...
...AND FOR YOUR COURAGEOUS LEADERSHIP UNDER ENEMY FIRE, I AM AWARDING YOU...
...YOUR OWN SHIP AND FIGHTER GROUP. YOUR CLONE FORCES ARE TO BE COMMENDED, CAPTAIN.
WITH THE ADDITION OF THE KHORMIAN AGROCITE TO OUR ARSENAL, I AM CONFIDENT WE HAVE TAKEN A BOLD STEP TOWARD BRINGING PEACE TO THE GALAXY. YOUR BRAVE SERVICE TO THE REPUBLIC MADE THIS GREAT VICTORY POSSIBLE.

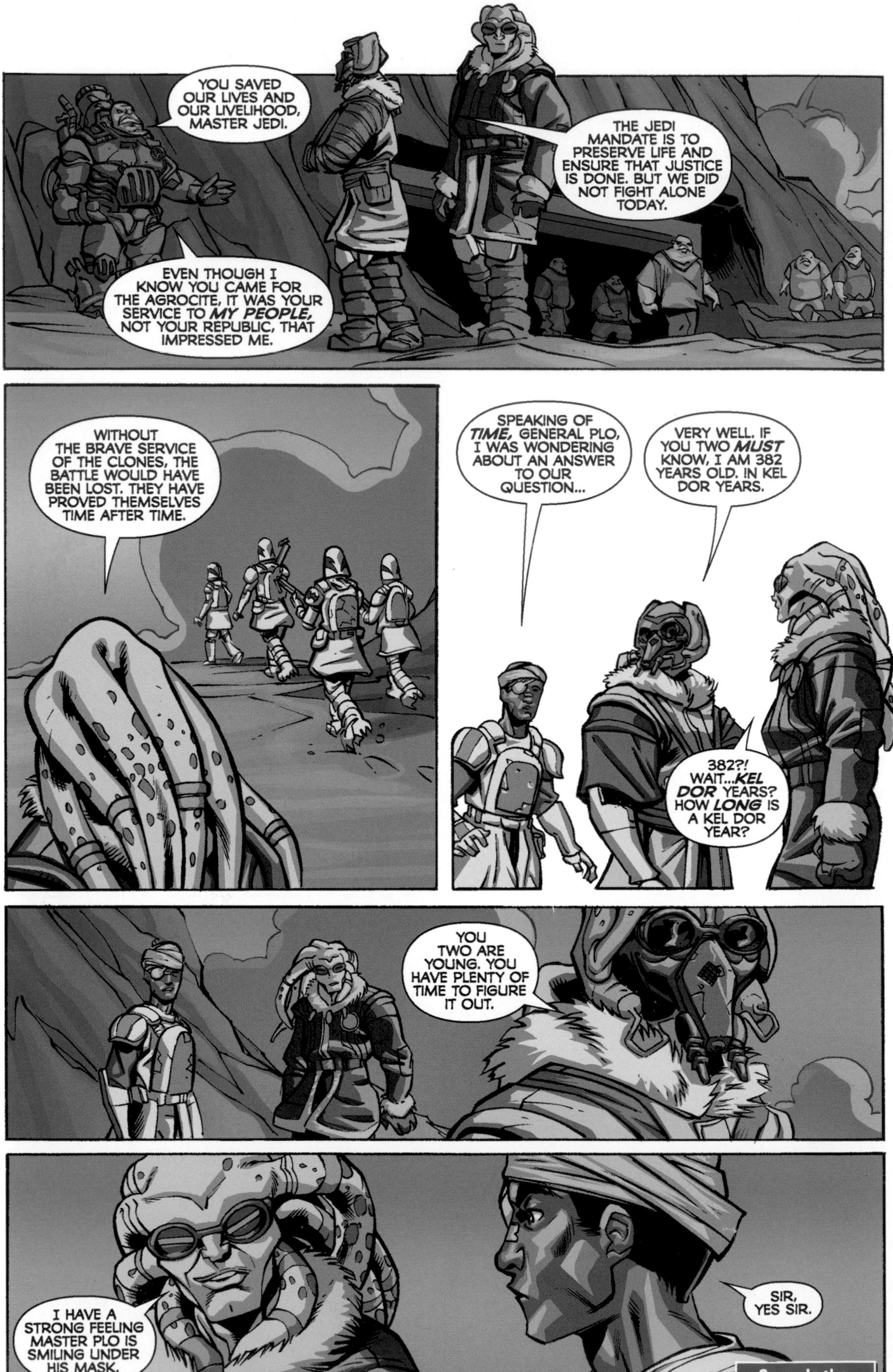
YOU SAVED OUR LIVES AND OUR LIVELIHOOD, MASTER JEDI.
THE JEDI MANDATE IS TO PRESERVE LIFE AND ENSURE THAT JUSTICE IS DONE. BUT WE DID NOT FIGHT ALONE TODAY.
EVEN THOUGH I KNOW YOU CAME FOR THE AGROCITE, IT WAS YOUR SERVICE TO MY PEOPLE, NOT YOUR REPUBLIC, THAT IMPRESSED ME.
WITHOUT THE BRAVE SERVICE OF THE CLONES, THE BATTLE WOULD HAVE BEEN LOST. THEY HAVE PROVED THEMSELVES TIME AFTER TIME.
SPEAKING OF TIME, GENERAL PLO, I WAS WONDERING ABOUT AN ANSWER TO OUR QUESTION...
VERY WELL. IF YOU TWO MUST KNOW, I AM 382 YEARS OLD. IN KEL DOR YEARS.
382?! WAIT...KEL DOR YEARS? HOW LONG IS A KEL DOR YEAR?
YOU TWO ARE YOUNG. YOU HAVE PLENTY OF TIME TO FIGURE IT OUT.
I HAVE A STRONG FEELING MASTER PLO IS SMILING UNDER HIS MASK.
SIR, YES SIR.
So ends the Battle of Khorm.